Where on Earth do animals live?

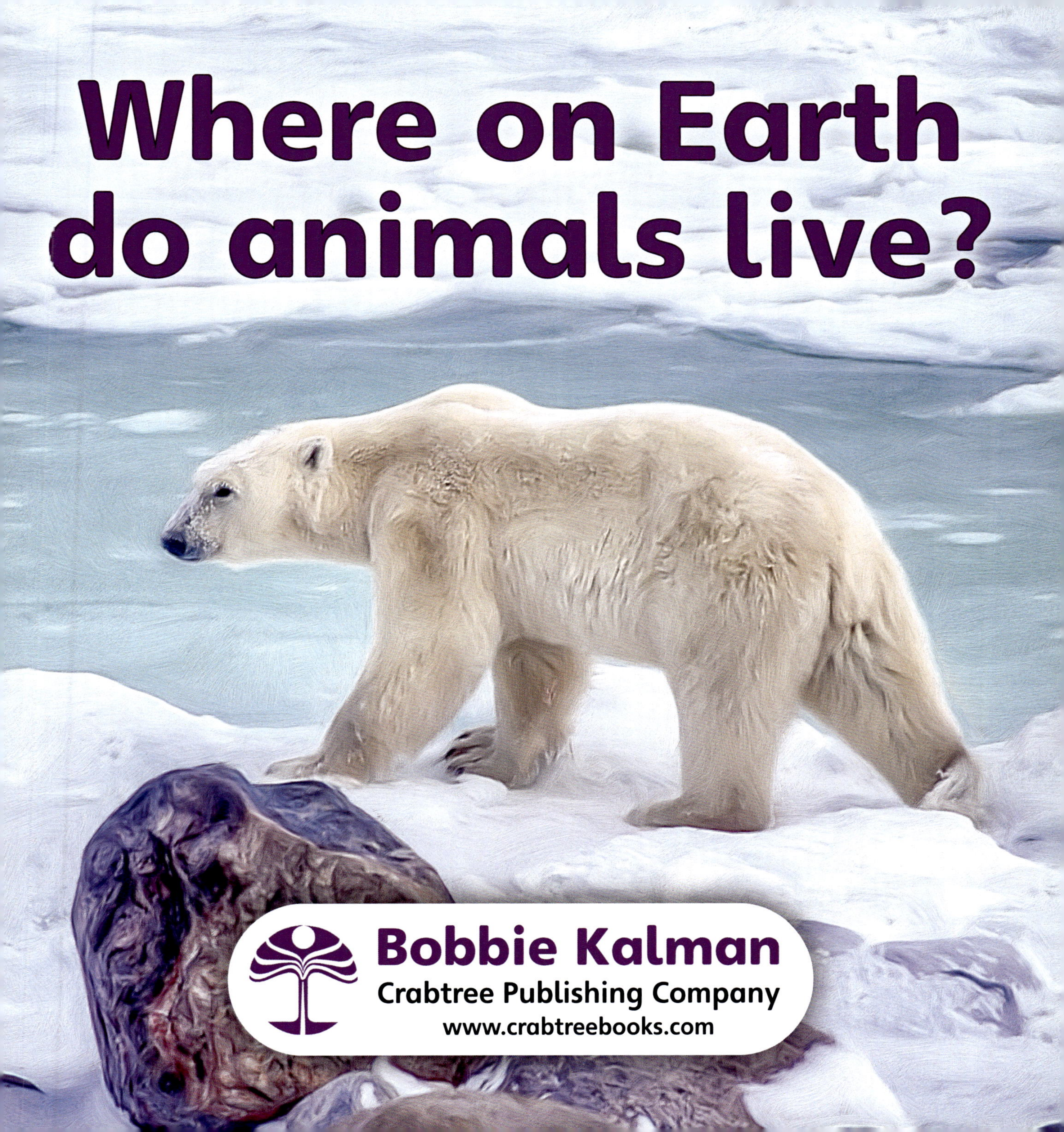

Bobbie Kalman

Crabtree Publishing Company
www.crabtreebooks.com

Created by Bobbie Kalman

For beautiful Eileen Zorko,
who loves to read, explore, and learn new things.
Your mother, Rhiannon, tells me that you love my books.

Author
Bobbie Kalman

Editor
Kathy Middleton

Educational consultants
Jennifer King
Janine Deschenes
Reagan Miller

Photo research
Bobbie Kalman

Design
Bobbie Kalman
Katherine Berti
Samantha Crabtree (cover)

Print coordinator
Katherine Berti

Illustrations
Barbara Bedell: p. 15 (top)

Photographs
Thinkstock: Yulia–Avgust: p. 23 (middle right)
Cover and all other images by Shutterstock

Library and Archives Canada Cataloguing in Publication

Kalman, Bobbie, author
Where on Earth do animals live? / Bobbie Kalman.

(My world)
Includes index.
Issued in print and electronic formats.
ISBN 978-0-7787-9601-5 (hardcover).
ISBN 978-0-7787-9609-1 (softcover).
ISBN 978-1-4271-1982-7 (HTML)

1. Habitat (Ecology)--Juvenile literature. 2. Animal ecology--Juvenile literature. 3. Endangered species--Juvenile literature. I. Title. II. Series: My world (St. Catharines, Ont.)

QH541.14.K3655 2017 j591.7 C2017-905180-6
C2017-905181-4

Library of Congress Cataloging-in-Publication Data

Names: Kalman, Bobbie, author.
Title: Where on Earth do animals live? / Bobbie Kalman.
Description: New York, New York : Crabtree Publishing, (2018) | Series: My world | Includes index.
Identifiers: LCCN 2017057226 (print) | LCCN 2017058375 (ebook) | ISBN 9781427119827 (Electronic HTML) | ISBN 9780778796015 (reinforced library binding) | ISBN 9780778796091 (pbk.)
Subjects: LCSH: Habitat (Ecology)--Juvenile literature. | Animal behavior--Juvenile literature. | Adaptation (Biology)--Juvenile literature.
Classification: LCC QH541.14 (ebook) | LCC QH541.14 .K355 2018 (print) | DDC 577--dc23
LC record available at https://lccn.loc.gov/2017057226

Crabtree Publishing Company
www.crabtreebooks.com 1-800-387-7650

Printed in Canada/092023/CPC20230918

Published in Canada
Crabtree Publishing
616 Welland Ave.
St. Catharines, Ontario
L2M 5V6

Published in the United States
Crabtree Publishing
347 Fifth Ave
Suite 1402-145
New York, NY 10016

Published in the United Kingdom
Crabtree Publishing
Maritime House
Basin Road North, Hove
BN41 1WR

Published in Australia
Crabtree Publishing
Unit 3-5
Currumbin Court
Capalaba QLD 4157

Contents

Animals on Earth

Animals live all over the Earth. The natural places where they live are called **habitats**. Animals **adapt**, or become suited to, the habitats in which they live.

Earth's continents

Habitats can be found on every **continent**, or huge area of land on Earth. Earth's seven continents, from largest to smallest, are Asia, Africa, North America, South America, Antarctica, Europe, and Australia and Oceania. Not every animal lives on every continent.

In this book, you will learn about the habitats you see on this map.

Five oceans surround the continents. Name them as you count on one hand.

Why do animals adapt?

Animals adapt to find food, survive in hot, cold, or dry habitats, escape danger, and stay safe. The bodies of some animals change. Animals that live in cold habitats, for example, grow thick fur to stay warm. Other animals change the way they live. Squirrel monkeys, for example, learned long ago to climb trees to keep safe from **predators** in the forest. Predators are animals that hunt and eat other animals.

Many birds, such as Canada geese, fly to warmer places for the winter.

This fennec fox has long ears. Its ears allow heat to escape from its body so the fox can keep cool in its hot desert home.

How do you adapt?

Compare the way animals adapt with the way you do. In a few sentences, describe how you have adapted to changes in your life, such as:

- moving to a new home
- summer and winter changes
- joining different groups
- making friends with someone who does not speak the same language as you.

Hot desert habitats

Deserts are areas that get less than ten inches (25 cm) of rain or snow a year. They can be found on every continent. Some are hot, and some are freezing cold. The Sahara Desert in Africa is the biggest hot desert. Animals there have adapted to living with very little water.

Camels store fat in humps on their backs. Their bodies use the fat when food and water are hard to find.

Helping one another

Animals that live in deserts must find enough food and water to stay alive. Meerkats live in the Kalahari Desert in Africa, which has more plants and animals than the Sahara. They have adapted to desert life by living in large groups. They help one another find food, take care of babies, and guard their homes from predators.

This meerkat is standing on guard. When it sees a predator, the guard lets out a loud call to warn the others of danger.

Icy polar habitats

Polar bears, arctic foxes, and many other animals live in the Arctic, which is a very cold desert in the northern part of Earth. Their thick fur and fat keep them warm.

foxes in summer

Arctic foxes are dark gray in summer and white in winter. The color of their fur helps them hide from predators in each season.

fox in winter

Polar bears have developed large paws to keep them from slipping on snow.

Cold Antarctica

Antarctica is a continent in the southern part of Earth. Few people live in this cold desert, but it is home to many kinds of penguins.

Penguins are birds with wings, but they cannot fly. They use their wings to swim.

Hot or cold desert?

Make a chart, like this one, which compares hot and cold deserts.

	Hot desert	*Cold desert*
Is there sand or snow?		
Which animals live there?		
How do their bodies keep warm or cool?		

Mountain animals

Mountains are areas of rocky land that rise high above the ground. Most mountains have steep sides. Trees and other plants grow on mountains, except at the very tops.

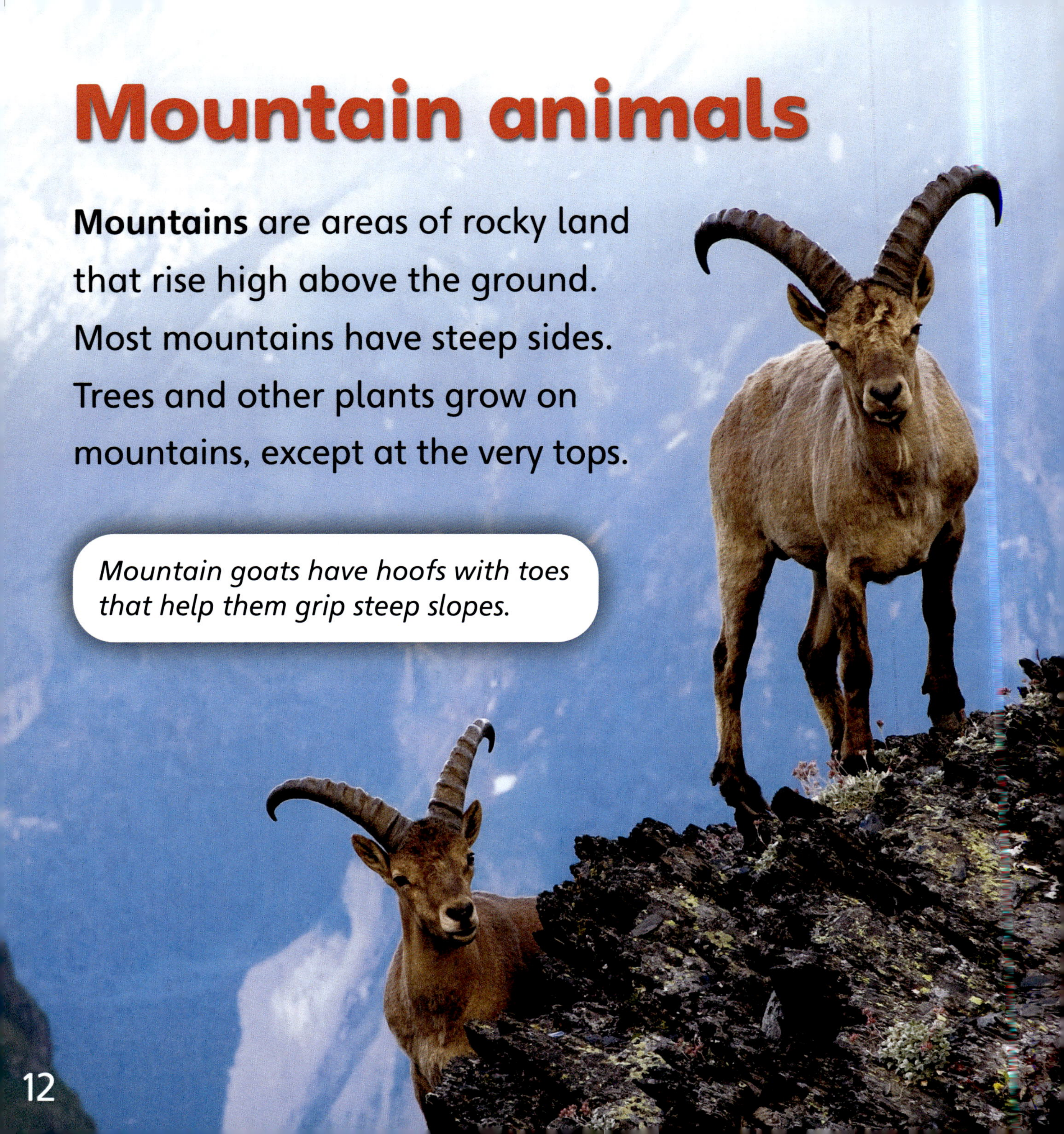

Mountain goats have hoofs with toes that help them grip steep slopes.

Be creative!

Mountain lions, mountain goats, bears, wolves, yaks, and guanacos are a few of the animals that live on mountains. Draw a picture or write a poem about your favorite mountain animal.

Different forests

A **forest** is a habitat where many trees and other plants grow. Some forests are in parts of the world where the weather is always hot and it rains every day. These forests are called **rain forests**.

The Amazon rain forest

The Amazon rain forest in South America is the biggest rain forest in the world. It has many kinds of birds, monkeys, and other animals.

Beautiful birds like this parrot live in the Amazon rain forest. They eat seeds, fruits, and leaves.

Northern forests

Although forests do not grow in cold areas such as the Arctic and Antarctica, there are many forests in the northern parts of Earth. Trees with needles and cones grow in these forests.

How many black bears can you see in this tree?

Mixed forests

Mixed forests have trees with flat leaves, as well as trees with needles. They grow in parts of the Earth that have four seasons. Flat leaves change color and drop off in autumn, but trees with needles stay green even in winter.

The animals on this page live in mixed forests.

Grassland habitats

Grasslands are areas where grasses, small plants, and a few trees grow. In areas with four seasons, grasslands are called **plains** or **prairies**. Many kinds of animals live in grasslands, where there is plenty of food to eat.

All these animals live in grasslands. Do you know which one lives only in Australia?

Draw or paint your own picture of a savanna. Don't forget to add some animals that live there.

Savanna animals

Savannas are large grasslands in areas that have only a wet season and a dry season. Some trees also grow there. Animals that live on the savannas in Africa include giraffes, elephants, zebras, cheetahs, gazelles, and lions. Some savanna animals eat only plants, and some hunt and eat other animals.

Ocean habitats

An **ocean** is a huge area of water that contains a lot of salt. Earth has five oceans. They are called Pacific, Atlantic, Indian, Southern, and Arctic. Different habitats are found in different oceans. Many animals live in warm oceans. Only certain animals can live in oceans that are covered in ice for part or all of the year.

Sea turtles, dolphins, and many kinds of fish live in warm oceans.

Freshwater habitats

Unlike ocean water, fresh water does not contain a lot of salt. Lakes, ponds, rivers, streams, and most **wetlands** are filled with fresh water. Wetlands are covered in water for all or part of the year. Ponds and lakes are areas of water with land all around them. The animals in freshwater habitats, such as alligators and frogs, often live in both water and on land.

Alligators live in wetlands.

Frogs lay their eggs in ponds.

Animals on islands

An **island** is an area of land that has water all around it. Islands are found all over the world in oceans, rivers, and lakes. Certain islands have animals that cannot be found anywhere else on Earth because animals on islands cannot move to new homes. Islands are surrounded by water and are often far from other places.

These animals both live only in Madagascar, an island that is part of Africa.

Endangered animals

If an animal is **endangered**, it means that it might soon disappear from Earth forever. Many island animals are endangered because their natural homes are being destroyed by people.

These animals live on islands in Asia. Both are endangered.

Fun activities

You will remember much more about animals and their habitats when you do some activities. Try the ones on this page and have fun learning!

Tell a classmate about this book. Make a list of the pages that have the important parts you want to teach to your classmate.

Make up some questions about information you've learned in this book. Then give your quiz to a classmate so he or she can find the answers in the book.

Describe the kinds of habitats near you. Which animals live there?

Words to know and Index

Notes for adults

Objectives
To teach children:
- Where animals live on a map of Earth's continents
- How to distinguish between different habitats
- Why and how animals adapt
- Nonfiction text features such as bold text, italics, bullets, captions, pictures, maps, etc.

Before Reading
- Read the title to the children and show them a few pages. Ask them what they think the book will be about.
- Give the children sticky notes to jot down key words after they read each section.

During Reading
- Have the children pause and talk about what they are learning.
- Have the children do a five-finger retell of the facts from the section they are reading. Each finger should represent a fact, and the palm of the hand should represent the big idea of the section.

After Reading
- Ask the children to jot down the names of the habitats on the map on pages 4 and 5. Then, see if they can name the animal that appears in each habitat picture.
- Ask them to share the parts of the book about which they had questions.
- Ask the children to identify nonfiction text features in the book. How did the text features help them learn?
- Ask them to identify the big ideas in each section of the book.

Discussion Points
- Ask the children to identify which habitat they think would be the most challenging for the animals that live there. Guide them to support their answers with evidence they found in this book.
- Invite them to discuss which animal they think could live in several habitats. What reasons did they give for their choice?

A Habitat Diagram
Ask the children to sketch a diagram of a habitat and list and label its parts.

Amazing Adaptations
Ask the children to choose one of the animals in this book and tell a partner about how it has adapted to its habitat. Guide the children by providing them with the following question prompts:
- Where does the animal live?
- Did it adapt to heat, cold, or lack of water?
- In which two ways does its body help it stay alive?
- How have you adapted to big changes in your life that are the same or different from the animal's adaptations?